D0720755

DAVE KEANE

Joe Sherlock

KID DETECTIVE

Case #000005:

The Art Teacher's Vanishing Masterpiece

HarperCollinsPublishers

Joe Sherlock, Kid Detective, Case #000005:
The Art Teacher's Vanishing Masterpiece
Copyright © 2007 by David J. Keane
Children's Books, a division of HarperCollins
Publishers, 1350 Avenue of the Americas, New York,
NY 10019.
www.harpercollinschildrens.com

Library of Congress Cataloging-in-Publication Data is
available.
ISBN-10: 0-06-085471-5 (pbk bdg.)
ISBN-13: 978-0-06-085471-3 (pbk bdg.)

1 2 3 4 5 6 7 8 9 10
❖
First Edition

For Tom Alessandri,
the best teacher I ever had.
—D.K.

Contents

• Chapter 1 •
The World Is a Stage

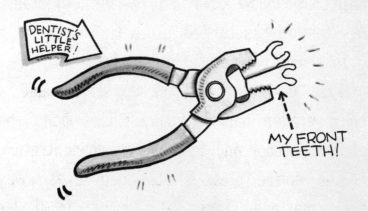

DENTIST'S LITTLE HELPER!

MY FRONT TEETH!

Before I say anything else, you should know right up front that I'm absolutely terrified to speak in front of more than two people at a time.

I'd rather have my two front teeth pulled out with a rusty pair of pliers than stand up in front of my class and give an oral report.

But that's exactly where I find myself, when my life takes an unexpected turn.

As I croak through my carefully memorized introduction, my legs feel like stale bread sticks. My heart feels like a red water balloon bouncing down a long flight of stairs. My tongue has turned into a fur coat.

In short, I'm not feeling so hot.

Just as I start to pick up some speed, a third grader named Jimmy Chee opens the classroom door and destroys my concentration.

The entire class shifts their eyes away from me and stares at Jimmy, as if his appearance is the most amazing thing to happen since the invention of the waffle iron.

Jimmy hands my teacher, Miss Piffle, a note. Every eye in the place follows the little scrap of paper like it's my death warrant. Jimmy gives me a long, strange look and backs out the doorway without a word.

Every eye in the class rotates back in my direction at the same time, like some kind of monster with fifty-three sleepy eyeballs.

Oh, no!

Maybe I'm distracted by Jimmy Chee's creepy stare. Or I'm too curious about the contents of that note. Perhaps it's the fact

THE NOTE

FIGHT IGNERINCE

that I can't remember if I zipped up my zipper this morning. Who knows? The only thing I know for sure is that all the words I've worked so hard to memorize are suddenly gone. Lost in space. Missing in action. Gone with the wind.

For a moment I think I might get a nosebleed from sheer panic.

Then I remember the index cards I have squeezed in my damp fist. My little sister, Hailey, suggested I write my speech out on note cards in case I fainted, threw up, or just freaked out in general—they don't call her a genius for nothing!

But there's a problem: When I flatten the index cards, I moan in horror when I realize these are not my cards at all! They're index cards detailing all the boys my big sister, Jessie, thinks are cute. *What on earth?*

"You'll have to stop right there, Sherlock,"

Miss Piffle says. She's staring at the note with a soaring eyebrow. "I'm afraid you need to leave right now."

"Thank you," I whisper.

Although I don't realize it yet, my fifth case as a private detective has finally arrived. Good thing, too, because I was about to fake my own death.

Miss Piffle,
Send Sherlock
to the office!
Make it snappy!
Your Boss,
The Principal

"Is this about the incident with the burning curtains?" I whisper to Miss Piffle with a sad, trembling voice. "It wasn't my fault!"

"What burning curtains incident?" she snaps, her face transforming instantly from concern to suspicion.

"Never mind," I mumble, desperate for some way to change the subject. "Maybe my parents are trying to get ahold of me. They went to Las Vegas for a few days to relax, gamble, and get away from me and my annoying sisters."

Miss Piffle seems to file this tidbit of information away for later use, probably at the next parent-teacher conference. "I have no earthly idea what the problem is," she sniffs. "It just says you are to report to the office immediately."

"Oh, sure," I say with a crooked smile. But my upset stomach tells another story: Any time you're yanked out of class in the middle of your first oral report, it probably isn't for *splendid* news.

"Before you go, we should discuss something," Miss Piffle says, arching the twin caterpillars she uses for eyebrows. "Your biographical report appears to be about Sherlock Holmes. Are you aware that Sherlock Holmes is a fictional character?"

POOFY DOO

LOOK OF DISAPPOINTMENT

UNIBROW

MYSTERY NOTE

I ♥ TESTS

MISS PIFFLE

"That's what I like best about him," I peep, although I'm really thinking that I have no earthly idea what the word "fictional" means.

To be perfectly honest, my teacher has what's called a unibrow, which means her eyebrows connect in the middle above her nose. So her eyebrows look like one long, hairy snake. It makes concentrating nearly impossible.

Miss Piffle can read my mind like an extremely short book. The hairy snake goes wild.

"Class, can anyone tell Sherlock what the word 'fictional' means?" Miss Piffle calls out.

After what feels like several million seconds, Sharon Sheldon speaks up. "'Fictional' means not real. A fictional character is made up, like for a book or movie."

"Thank you, Sharon," Miss Piffle beams proudly.

"Whatever," I hear Sharon Sheldon sigh from behind me. She's one of the smartest, most popular kids at Baskerville Elementary School, but her big brother is a gorilla who just happens to wear pants.

Miss Piffle sinks the caterpillars as low as they'll go.

I know this look; she's about to drop the hammer on me. "As a result of this breaking news, Sherlock, you will have to find another character to do your oral report on, preferably someone who actually lived and breathed."

"Hey, why don't you do your oral report on Inspector Wink-Wink?" my best friend, Lance Peeker, booms through the silence. Of course, as with anything Lance says, the class explodes with laughter, like I just sat on one of those farting whoopee cushions while getting hit in the face with a banana cream pie.

I feel more like I've been hit in the stomach with a park bench.

How could the world's greatest detective, my hero, The Great Detective himself, not be real? There are thousands of movies about him—and I have almost every one of them!

I somehow manage to snatch the note out of Miss Piffle's hand and stumble out through the classroom door.

The eyebrow waves good-bye.

I gulp at the air, fanning my face with the tiny note. My wobbly legs steer me toward the school's office.

"Hey, my note worked."

It's my little sister, Hailey. She grabs the

note, shakes her head, and tosses the note into a nearby garbage can.

"You mean that note was fake?" I gasp.

"It wasn't fake! I really wrote it," Hailey informs me with a shrug. She starts pulling me down the empty hallway. "Sometimes a lie isn't a lie, especially when being untruthful is meant to uncover a deeper truth," she says.

My sister always throws these verbal obstacle courses at me to distract me. They work. As my brain gropes its way through the mental maze, I forget what had me so flipped out in the first place.

Instantly, the tension begins to drain from my scrunched-up forehead.

Then I see a police car waiting at the curb outside the office!

"Holy hot sauce! They know about the burning curtains incident! They're coming to take me away! Quick, hide me in a garbage can!"

"Whoa! Take it easy!" Hailey yells, holding me by the back of my pants so I can't dive headfirst into a garbage can. "What burning curtains incident?"

"Never mind," I snarl between clenched teeth. "The less you know, the better."

"Hey, that's your approach to life, not mine," she shoots back.

I spin around, but the expression on Hailey's face stops me cold.

She stands, arms crossed, a look of genuine concern in her eyes. "Wait a minute," she whispers. "This isn't about burning curtains, is it? You're an odd shade of pea green. What happened? Oh, no . . . was Irene Adler picking and eating another one of her scabs?"

For a brief moment I think my lunch might come up for a victory lap. That tuna fish sandwich didn't look so good *before* it went down, so I really doubt it would win any beauty contests in its current condition.

"Is Sherlock Holmes a 'fractional' character?" I blurt out.

"'Fractional'? I think you mean 'fictional,'" she replies evenly. "Look, I didn't want to say anything," she continues, shifting uncomfortably. "Sherlock Holmes is not real. Okay? He never was. He's just a character created for some magazine stories over a hundred years ago. Sorry."

My lower lip quivers. My eyeballs feel like they're doing figure eights in my skull. The air seems to have gone mountain-peak thin.

"Hey, I'm sorry for your loss, but you need to snap out of it," Hailey says, stabbing a finger in my chest. "The cop that's parked out front is Officer Lestrade. He's looking for you. And not because you torched some window coverings. Mrs. Bagby, our very own art teacher, had a valuable painting ripped off last night. Lestrade asked me to get you out of class. He needs your help. Now. As in extra pronto with a cherry on top and a police cruiser at the curb."

I'm still in shock over the disturbing news about my hero. But my fifth official case as a private detective just fell into my lap like a very large bowling ball. And it feels great!

I notice I'm no longer gasping for breath. I'm once again sucking in air like a champ. "Let's go crack us a case," I say with a nod.

"Great," Hailey replies. "But before we interview Mrs. Bagby, you might want to zip up your zipper."

• Chapter 4 •
Art Teacher Toast

Our school's office makes me feel itchy, nervous, and guilty for reasons I haven't been able to figure out yet.

But Hailey? She just loves the place. Heck, she thinks it's more fun than a barrel of apes.

"Why didn't you just have Officer Lestrade ask Principal Lupin to get me out of class?" I ask.

"Sherlock, just let me do what I do best,

and you do what you do best," she says. "Besides, we don't have time for permission slips, parental approvals, and small talk."

In case you're wondering why my little sister gets to walk around like she owns the place, it's because she's the only second grader on the planet with a free period. She gets a free period for math because she takes a high school geometry class. In short, my little sister is too smart for her own good.

As we enter a room strangely labeled TEACHER'S LOUNGE, PLEASE NO FLASH PHOTOGRAPHY, I can tell instantly that something is amiss, which is just Sherlock Holmes's uppity way of saying "messed up bad."

My eyes sweep over a microwave oven that's seen one too many beef enchiladas, a chalkboard showing the number of days left till summer vacation, several dozen bottles of assorted pain relievers, and an oxygen tank.

Mrs. Bagby is flat on her back on the couch like a slice of sofa toast, groaning loudly and covered with a splotchy red rash.

Although Mrs. Bagby is usually covered with a splotchy red rash, I notice she is currently breaking her personal splotch record.

Mrs. Bagby visits every class at Baskerville

Elementary School once a week to teach squirming kids about art history. I must admit it's a tough crowd. And she seems to think all the groaning, yawning, and burping means the kids don't like her. But the sad truth is, most kids don't give a ham sandwich about art.

"Mrs. Bagby, my brother's here," Hailey says in a sweet and caring voice she never uses with me.

I notice Mrs. Bagby has kicked off her shoes. I've never seen a teacher's feet before, and the sight of her plump toes makes me feel uncomfortable and a bit panicky.

Mrs. Bagby blinks in my direction with unfocused, glossy eyes. "You're the boy in Miss

Piffle's class who fidgets constantly," she says unsteadily. "Your sister tells me you're a mystery solver. Is that right?"

"I'm much better at solving mysteries than I am at art history," I say awkwardly.

"Well that's not saying much. You're getting a C- in Art," she sighs, dabbing at her eyes with a tissue. She's quiet for a moment, gathering her thoughts. "An extremely rare and valuable painting that's hung in my living room for the last thirty-five years was stolen last night from the Baskerville Museum of Art, History, and Walnut Farming."

I know the place she's talking about. My class recently took our field trip there, and we were forced to learn more about growing walnuts than a kid should ever have to.

"Why wasn't the painting in your living room?" I ask.

"I had finally decided to sell it," Mrs.

Bagby says to the ceiling in a cracking and quivering voice. "The museum is hosting Baskerville's first annual art auction tonight. I dropped it off just yesterday with tears in my eyes. The money I would have gotten for selling it was going to fund my retirement. Now it's been stolen." She turns her watery eyes in my direction. "You seem like the type of person who needs to write things down."

"Um . . . I forgot my backpack in my classroom," I say.

"That's exactly what I'm talking about," Mrs. Bagby mumbles.

"Don't worry, Mrs. Bagby; unlike my brother, I don't forget things," Hailey says, shaking her head at me.

Before I can ask another question, Officer Lestrade pokes his head into the room. "Sherlock, there you are! I just came from your classroom. If you want to see that crime scene, I've got to take you over there now. The auction is set to begin in just three hours, and the clock is ticking."

I consider the fact that my entire class must think I'm being hunted by the police.

I bet Miss Piffle's eyebrow went bananas.

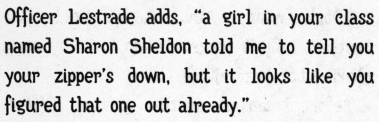

"Oh, and Sherlock," Officer Lestrade adds, "a girl in your class named Sharon Sheldon told me to tell you your zipper's down, but it looks like you figured that one out already."

Spending the rest of my life hiding under my bed is looking better every minute.

• Chapter 5 •
Passing the Smell Test

Lucky for my stomach, the traffic is slow on the Baskerville Expressway. Unlucky for my stomach, the backseat of Officer Lestrade's police car smells like a poorly run petting zoo.

Hailey doesn't seem too wild about the wet-elephant smell either. "Does this stink bomb come equipped with oxygen masks? I'm ready to confess to something just to get a whiff of fresh air."

"I'd roll down your window if I could," Officer Lestrade says with a shrug.

Amazingly, the stench doesn't seem to bother Officer Lestrade. I figure the hideous odor must have long ago blackened and dried up the inside of his nostrils just like roofing tar.

"Maybe we should stop at the next drugstore and get some gas-powered air fresheners," Hailey suggests.

"I called your house back at the school," Officer Lestrade chuckles through the two-inch-thick slab of glass that separates him from the bad guys he arrests. "I spoke with your grandfather. He's quite a character."

See, when somebody calls a relative of yours a "character," it's basically a code word for saying that the person seems like a complete nutcase. It's safe to say everyone in my family exceeds the legal limit in the "character" department.

"So, have you ever shot anybody?" Hailey hollers through the glass.

"Hailey!" I gasp. "That's rude!"

"No, I've never shot anybody," Officer Lestrade says slowly.

Hailey seems to slump in disappointment. "What kind of heat are you packing anyway? Your gun looks like an old revolver. Talk about a dinosaur! Why don't you carry a nine millimeter? They carry fifteen rounds in a clip with one in the chamber, and they're much faster to reload."

The squad car goes silent. Officer Lestrade shifts uncomfortably in his seat, as I'm sure he's thanking his lucky stars he's on *that* side of the bulletproof glass.

"The Baskerville police department has had its budget cut for the last five years in a row," Officer Lestrade explains. "New equipment takes a backseat to gas money and paychecks."

While Hailey and Officer Lestrade discuss the finer points of body armor, pepper spray, and the history of the nightstick, I take Mrs.

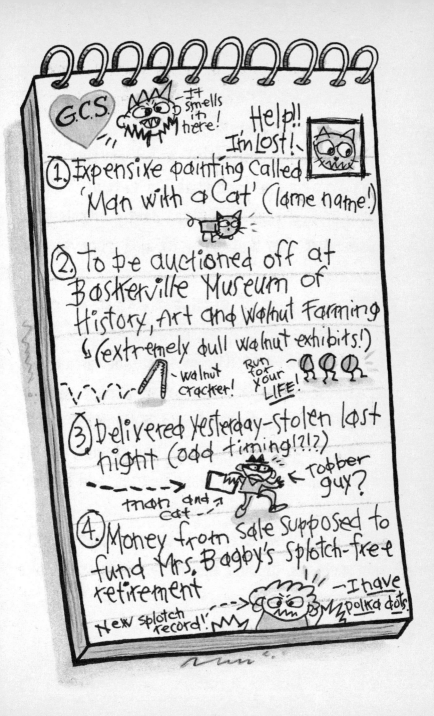

Bagby's advice and jot down what I know so far, on a Girl Chat Sleepover notepad I borrow from Hailey.

My notes cover all I know at this point. There's also the fact that I'm getting paid my regular day rate, and Mrs. Bagby promised to raise my C– in Art to a B+ if I recover the stolen artwork.

The prospect of getting my first B+ gives me a little boost of extra excitement.

"We're here," Officer Lestrade announces as the squad car comes to an abrupt stop in an alley between two large buildings.

That's when I notice Hailey staring at me with a combination of fear, disgust, and horror.

"What?" I ask innocently.

"It's not this car. . . . It's you that stink!" she screams, holding her nose. "You smell like gross dog farts!"

• Chapter 6 •
Shirt Invaders

Hailey's right.

I'm wearing my favorite shirt, and it smells like a dirty diaper.

"Dang it!" I gag, sliding out of the police cruiser when Officer Lestrade gets around to opening my door. I pull the reeking shirt over my head, walk over to a Dumpster, lift the lid a few inches, and toss the hideous thing in.

"Fire in the hole!" Hailey shouts to

nobody in particular.

Already the smell of rotting vegetables starts to fade.

Now the four of us—Hailey, Lestrade, and my nipples—stand around staring at one another, not sure what to do next.

Finally Hailey turns to Officer Lestrade. "Did you know this is National Skinny Brother Awareness Month?"

I give her an icy glare that would surely melt wood, but she just smiles. Even I must admit, I'm slightly less impressive bare chested.

The reason my shirt stinks like something that died several months ago is no mystery. The culprit is Man Laundry.

Man Laundry is my dad's brilliant idea to help out with the housework. He promised to wash my laundry and his laundry together once a week to lighten my mom's workload. The problem is, he starts the washing machine on Friday night and doesn't remember to throw our twisted and stiff clothes into the dryer until late Sunday night, after our moist

MILDEW FARM

MAN LAUNDRY

laundry has rotted in the dark for more than fifty-eight hours, growing heaps of mildew.

The nasty thing about mildew is that it smells when you warm it up, like putting a plate of dead chipmunks in a microwave oven and hitting the Pot Roast button.

"Follow me," Officer Lestrade coughs, obviously holding in a good laugh at my expense. We follow him to the museum's locked front doors. "I told the museum's curator I'd call him when we got here," he says, punching buttons on his cell phone.

"I bet you don't know what a curator is," Hailey teases me.

"Of course I do," I say unconvincingly. "It's someone who cures things."

"It's the person in charge of the artwork at a museum," Officer Lestrade says, trying to save me from the world's most annoying little sister.

"Uh-oh," Hailey says, tapping me on my bare backbone. She points to a sign on the door that reads: NO SHOES. NO SHIRT. NO SERVICE. "You'll just have to wait in the car," she says with a shrug. "So, are you going to go quietly? Or are we going to have to cuff you?"

There's nothing easy about having a little sister. There's also nothing easy about solving mysteries. And as I'm about to find out, things are about to get even more uneasy for the half-naked detective.

NO SHOES
SHIRT
SERVICE

NO EXCUSES. NO EXCEPTIONS. NO KIDDING.

• Chapter 7 •
Crime in a Box

"Sorry, but the waterslide is not working today," sneers a strange-looking man who pokes his head out through the museum door.

I think he's making a snarky joke about my current state of bare-chestedness. But I can't be certain, because his eerie face is unmoving and lifeless, like a brick with a nose.

Then it hits me: He looks like one of those giant stone heads on Easter Island.

My class learned about Easter Island's ancient and mysterious stone blockheads in our reading comprehension workbooks. Apparently, some ancient guys carved hundreds of these giant heads on a grassy island out in the middle of the ocean a few million years ago. I distinctly remember not comprehending much of the story.

EASTER ISLAND HEADS

"I'll be right back," Stone Head sniffs after Officer Lestrade pleads his case for letting in a shirtless kid detective and his walking headache of a little sister.

He returns in moments and hands me a purple T-shirt. In enormous letters the shirt screams I LOVE ART!

"Does it have to be a lady's T-shirt?" I groan.

"It's the cheapest shirt on the gift shop's clearance table," Stone Head sighs.

"Does it have to be purple?" I murmur.

"That's lavender," Stone Head corrects me. "And rules are rules."

Hailey's having the time of her life watching me suffer. "At least it doesn't smell like a sewage treatment plant," she says, pulling the shirt over my head. "Oh, Sherlock, you could be in a little detective fashion show!"

"Follow me," Stone Head orders us.

We follow his enormous forehead up a wide wooden staircase and to the entrance of the auction room. There is a yellow plastic strip strung tightly across the doorway. It says CRIME SCENE on it every five inches or so. That is so cool.

Before I can stop her, Hailey runs in slow motion through the yellow tape, her arms raised in the air, like she's winning a marathon. The tape snaps. She makes the sound of a roaring crowd. "Hailey Sherlock has shocked the world and taken the gold medal!" she shouts like a TV announcer.

Stone Head doesn't look amused.

I walk slowly around the auction room and get a feel for the place.

I count nineteen paintings of various sizes hanging neatly around the room. There is one empty space. I stare at the tiny hole in the wall that only yesterday was occupied by the hook holding Mrs. Bagby's painting. I wonder what kind of thief steals a painting *and* the hook it's hanging on.

I stare at that hole for a long time.

When I turn around, everyone is looking at me like I just kicked a sleeping dog. And I must admit, this case is starting to feel like one.

I find myself sitting all alone in the auction room of the museum waiting for a brilliant idea to drop out of the sky and hit me on the head like a falling coconut. But nothing happens.

I've taken several laps around this room. I've seen the narrow broken window just wide enough for Mrs. Bagby's painting to have been slipped through sideways. I've spotted the shattered glass in the alley down below in front of Officer Lestrade's police cruiser. I've also studied the remaining nineteen paintings, checked the high ceiling for skylights (none!), and considered the fact that this room has only one way in, or out.

I can't help but think that maybe the painting just got stolen, and it's gone for good, and there's nothing I can do about it, and Mrs. Bagby will have to continue to teach those yawning, burping kids about dull art for twenty more years.

I pull Hailey's Girl Chat Sleepover pad out of my pocket and flip to a new page, thinking that writing down my puzzlements may calm the mad scramble going on in my head.

Which reminds me of my disastrous oral report from earlier in the day.

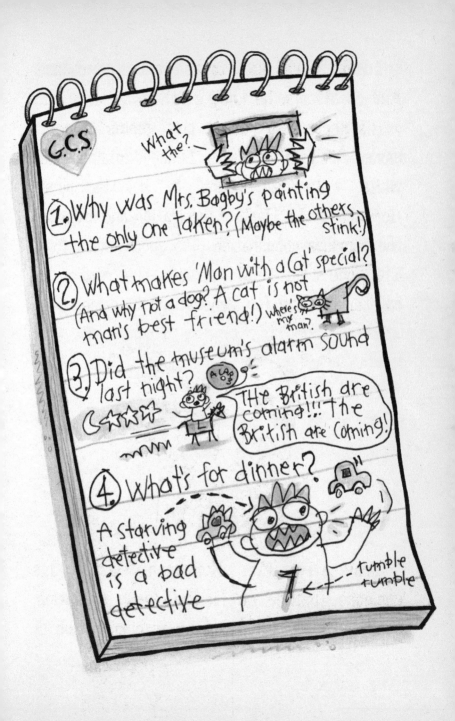

I had the bad luck to go right after Lance. And as always, he knocked their socks off.

His report was about this genius inventor named Spencer Horgarth. Lance explained that while tinkering around in his basement, Horgarth had a flash of inspiration and invented the spork, a combination of a spoon and a fork. This one idea would change the course of cafeteria eating for generations to come.

The Spork!

Tragically, Mr. Horgarth wasted his immense fortune on his follow-up invention, the "spife," a highly unpopular combination of a spoon and a knife that left him bitter, penniless, and lonely.

At the conclusion of Lance's report, the class actually applauded. Sharon Sheldon even whistled. Miss Piffle's eyebrow made waves.

Then I shuffled to the front of the class to start my report on a guy who never actually lived—with my zipper down and my favorite shirt smelling of rotting pumpkins.

"Hey, Sherlock!" Hailey suddenly shouts, breaking the silence like a bull in a china shop. "Why don't we look at the video from the security cameras?"

"That sounds promising," I say, kicking myself for not thinking of it first. This may be the coconut I was waiting for!

Sometimes you catch a break that's just too good to be true. And I had a suspicion this clue would fit that description like a glove.

"That camera is just for show," Stone Head explains, staring up at the cameras like he can't believe it himself. "City Hall slashed our budget during the installation of our security cameras. We never even got the wires to connect the cameras to anything. But they seem to fool just about everybody."

"Everyone but the thief," I think out loud. I wonder if the art thief knew ahead of time that he wouldn't be caught on camera. Was it just plain luck? Or am I dealing with an inside job? "Dang it! Finally, a coconut falls on my head and it's hollow!"

"We don't need a coconut to tell us that your head is hollow," Hailey mutters, staring up at the fake cameras.

"I've got to go!" Officer Lestrade announces abruptly from the stairs. "Something's up. I just got a call from the police chief himself. He wants a big sit-down for some reason."

"Boy, this sure is going to be interesting!" I exclaim.

"You kids will have to get a ride home," he says flatly.

"Oh," I say, deflating like a popped parade float.

"I've got it covered," Hailey assures him, pulling out our dad's cell phone. She gives me a wink, acknowledging the fact that our dad trusts her with his cell phone and not me. She turns back to Officer Lestrade. "You roll ten-nineteen. We'll be ten-eight here for a bit and call if we need a ten-sixteen. Just call us later with your nine-fifty-two."

Amazingly, Officer Lestrade seems to know what she's talking about. He nods crisply. "Ten-four," he replies, and is gone.

While Hailey calls our grandparents for a ride, I corner Stone Head and look over my list of questions. I give him my best detective glare and raise an eyebrow so high even Miss Piffle would be impressed. "What's so special about this painting?" I ask.

"There are only forty-three paintings by

this artist known to exist," he explains. "For years there has been a rumor about the existence of a forty-fourth, said to be the artist's masterpiece. And when I saw it, I agreed it was a major discovery. It was to be the star of this auction. The local art world is . . . *was* buzzing about the chance to acquire it."

"Does this place have a burglar alarm?" I ask quickly, trying to catch him off guard. "And if so, did it go off last night?"

"No alarms were triggered last night," he

sighs, looking around over my head like he's searching for someone more fun to talk to. "I would have been called at home if the alarm sounded. I arrived this morning to prepare for the auction, and I was greeted by this large, unseemly gap on the wall."

I'm not sure what "unseemly" means, but I decide to let that one go. I push on. "Any cars in the alley outside that window when you arrived?"

"No," he sniffs, managing a slight shake of his rocklike head. He must have a strong neck!

No cameras. Nobody in the alley. No alarms. No witnesses. Basically, I have nothing to work with. I try a new angle. "Anybody else have keys to this place? Somebody who could have come in last night and ripped off Mrs. Bagby's painting?"

"I have a set of keys, and so does Clem, our maintenance man for the last eleven years. He also knows the code to deactivate the alarm. But Clem did not come in last night, and there is no record of the alarm being turned off, which would be reflected on the computer printout I gave to the officer." He looks at his watch for a long time, like he's counting the seconds till I drop dead.

Something else occurs to me. "Doesn't the museum have insurance to pay for this kind of thing?"

"Ah, there's the rub," he says slowly.

"Okay, I was willing to let 'unseemly' go by, but what the heck is a 'rub'?" I grumble in frustration.

"What I mean is that your art teacher's painting was never authenticated," he explains. "*Man with a Cat* never received an official certificate of authenticity by an art appraiser who would certify—"

"That the painting was really created by

the artist," Hailey interrupts from directly behind me. I flinch. Sneaking up on me and scaring the living cheese out of me is surely her most maddening habit. "And without written proof that the painting was genuine," she continues, "I bet the insurance company will refuse to pony up a settlement to compensate Mrs. Bagby for any monetary losses caused by the burglary."

"That's what I was afraid of," I agree, trying my best to sound like I actually

understand all that jibber-jabber.

"Precisely," Stone Head says. "Now I really must get back to work, children. The museum's chairman is pressuring me to put this whole unfortunate episode behind us as quickly as possible. So I must ask you both to leave now."

Hailey starts pulling me by the arm. "C'mon, Sherlock, Grandpappy's picking us up in Bessie."

Hailey calls our grandpa "Grandpappy" because she knows it drives me absolutely crazy.

Sometimes I try to imagine a world without little sisters.

Bessie is what my grandpa calls his pile-of-junk old car that backfires so much you feel like you're riding in a shooting gallery. It also stalls out every time somebody looks at you funny—which happens a lot since that bucket of bolts backfires just about every time you blink.

"And Grandpappy's made his famous flat-rabbit stew for dinner," Hailey exclaims.

Famous? Famously disgusting is more like it!

Instantly, my stomach feels like it's full of ferrets. My neck gets sweaty. I think my gag reflex even fires off a few times before we reach the stairs.

Surely today could not get any worse!

"Wait! I'll need to get that shirt back before you leave," Stone Head calls after me.

"Oh, I thought you gave it to me," I say.

"No, that was just a loaner," he says with a sour voice. "And you may also want to know that your zipper's down."

"AGAIN! What the—oh, sorry about that," I say, yanking the zipper back up. "It must be broken."

If something actually goes right today, I may die from the shock.

FLAT RABBIT STEW?

Riding shirtless in the back of a noisy, convertible pile of junk doesn't exactly help me think—especially since this is my most complicated case yet.

The snarled Friday afternoon traffic is also getting us nowhere fast, so I better come up with something soon, considering the auction is now less than two hours away.

"So how's the detective business, Sherlock?"

my grandpa shouts back at me.

"Great!" I reply, but my response can't be heard because the tailpipe explodes with a large BLAM! just as I open my mouth. My grandpa nods anyway, satisfied with my unheard answer. Maybe this car has forced him to learn how to read lips.

I pull a small square sticker from my front pocket. I secretly peeled it off the wall next to the empty space recently occupied by Mrs.

Bagby's painting. I don't think they'll miss it. I study it for several minutes. I admit that the short list of facts doesn't seem to move me any closer to a solution, just one step closer to a throbbing headache.

I need what detectives in the movies call "background." Background is just a fancy way of saying you need to gather every fact you can lay your grubby hands on about the people, places, and things involved in your case.

Then I have an idea. "Grandpa, I need to swing by Lance's house," I shout over the sputtering engine. "Do you remember where his house is?"

He turns and says something, but I can't hear it because of another cannon blast from Bessie's exhaust pipe. I'm pretty sure he said, "Yes!" Look, now I'm learning to read lips, too.

I fold the sticker up and stuff it back in my pocket.

"What's your take on that snooty curator guy?" I ask Hailey. But the question just hangs in the air, unanswered. She's not really paying attention anymore. She's reading a book about shipwrecks that she pulled from her backpack. The truth is, Hailey seems to view my cases as mild amusements between books. Some assistant!

I'm struck by the fact that she just happens to be reading about shipwrecks, because this case is starting to give me a horrible sinking feeling.

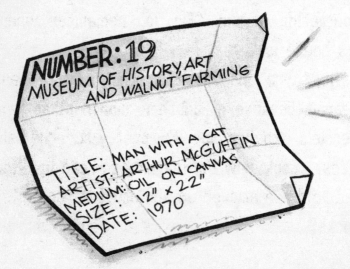

NUMBER: 19
MUSEUM OF HISTORY, ART AND WALNUT FARMING

TITLE: MAN WITH A CAT
ARTIST: ARTHUR McGUFFIN
MEDIUM: OIL ON CANVAS
SIZE: 12" x 22"
DATE: 1970

• Chapter 11 •
The Lance and Jimmy Show

"Hey, we all thought you got arrested," Lance chuckles when he finally opens his front door. "Did they take your shirt as evidence?"

"No, I haven't been arrested, I'm helping the police with a case," I say, bending the truth just a bit, thinking it might help me convince Lance to use his Internet skills to dig up some background for me.

"Man, you look like a stick figure wearing

shoes," Lance laughs.

"Just listen to what I have to say!" I demand. "Mrs. Bagby had a valuable painting ripped off last night at the museum downtown."

"I wasn't anywhere near that museum last night!" Lance snaps defensively.

"I don't think you took it, for heaven's sake!" I shout. "I just need something from you."

"Do you want some beef jerky or something?" he asks. "I think I can see your heart beating in your chest."

"Not exactly . . . ," I burble like an idiot, my mouth watering at the thought of food, even if it's the kind that tastes like dried-up squirrels.

"We need you to gather some background about Mrs. Bagby's painting and the artist on the Internet," Hailey says from just inches behind me. I try not to flinch, but my shoulders jump a little despite my best efforts.

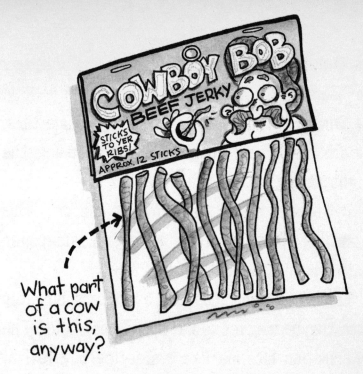

What part of a cow is this, anyway?

"Yeah, you're great at researching stuff," I say, trying to win him over. "Your report on the guy who invented the spork was amazing."

"I made that stuff up," he whispers, looking back over his shoulder. "I forgot to do the homework, and I thought my turn wouldn't come until Monday. So I thought up most of that stuff on the spot."

"You made up your report?" I gasp.

"Quiet!" Lance hisses. "I don't want Jimmy to hear."

"Jimmy?" Hailey and I ask at the same time.

"Oh, yeah . . . Jimmy Chee is spending the night at my house."

It takes me a moment to absorb this startling fact. "You're having a sleepover with Jimmy Chee?" I gulp.

Lance's grandma barely even lets me step into the house, let alone spend the night. The information hits me like a sleeping bag full of rocks. Lance has been my best friend since first grade, and he's never invited *me* to a sleepover!

Like a bad penny, Jimmy Chee appears behind Lance in the doorway.

Lance clearly notices the surprise on my face. "Jimmy's stepdad is having shoulder surgery today," he explains. "His mom asked my grandma if he could spend the night so his

dad can moan and
complain in peace
without some kid
irritating him
every second of
the day. Jimmy
can get under your
skin like nobody's
business."

"Did you know you forgot to put your shirt on?" Jimmy asks, proving Lance's point beautifully.

Nobody answers him. We stand frozen in awkward silence. You could cut the tension with a spork.

"We better get going," Hailey says, grabbing me by the shoulder. "We have a grandpappy waiting," she sneers at Lance and Jimmy.

"What the heck is a grandpappy?" Lance asks, truly confused.

"Will you help me?" I ask quietly, anxious to get back to my sinking ship but more anxious to get some background for my case.

Jimmy clears his throat. "Hey, I thought we were making snickerdoodles!"

"You're making cookies?" I ask in a voice that's similar to the hissing sound a beanbag makes when your fat uncle sits on it.

Hailey waves a hand in front of Lance's face. "Are you helping or not?"

"Okay," Lance grumbles, simply to put an end to the awkward tension between us. "I'll get started first thing in the morning."

"You've got sixty minutes," I say, handing him the folded-up sticker from the museum. I turn and head for Chitty Chitty Bang Bang.

Behind me I hear Hailey giving Lance our dad's cell phone number and Lance suggesting that he send over a couple dozen snickerdoodles to put some meat on my bones.

When Hailey finally joins me in the car, I breathe a sigh of relief. Just then the car

stalls and my grandpa can't get it to start again. As the engine hacks, gasps, and splutters at the curb, Lance and Jimmy Chee stand in the doorway, watching as my ship takes on more water. I wish Lance would stop staring and get to work on gathering background.

I sink in my seat.

I have so much more to do, and so much farther to sink, that I honestly don't think I'll know when I hit bottom.

• Chapter 12 •
A Picture Worth a Thousand Words

We leave our grandpa at the curb in front of Lance's house, mumbling curses under Bessie's hood. On the walk back down Baker Street, I work out a plan of action in my head. By the time I push through the front door of my house, I know exactly what to do.

Step one is putting on a shirt. I choose my lucky Inspector Wink-Wink shirt, which I don't wear much in public because it rattles people to see a kid in the fourth grade wearing a shirt about a TV show for first graders. But you can't please everybody.

Step two is tracking down every lead we've got. "Get on the phone and see if you can talk to Clem, the museum's janitor," I instruct Hailey when I find her reading on the couch.

"Nice shirt," she says with a grin. "Is every other shirt you own in the Man Laundry basket?"

See what I'm talking about!

"We need to know everyone who saw that painting yesterday," I continue. "And I don't trust that rock-headed curator as far as I can throw him, which wouldn't be far."

"You're not known for your muscle mass," Hailey says.

"And see if you can find out what happened to Officer Lestrade."

"Ten-four, Major Mildew," Hailey says, saluting.

"And call Lance and tell him we're almost out of time. I need him to find out the name of the museum's chairman."

"Anything else, boss?" she says. "Perhaps you want me to pick up all the dirty underwear in your room? Or pluck the fuzz ball out of your belly button?"

"I have a fuzz ball in my belly button?" I say, feeling around in there with a finger.

"Oh, you probably should see this," Hailey says, handing me an old, faded photograph.

"Grandma says Mrs. Bagby dropped it off earlier."

"Why didn't you say something?" I gasp, staring at the picture.

"Your shirt threw me for a loop," she says simply.

The photo shows a much younger Mrs. Bagby, a tall older man, a bearded man wearing a headband and round sunglasses, and a corner of a painting, which I assume is *Man with a Cat*. The rest of the painting is cut off, but at least I can see a corner.

GRANDMA SHERLOCK

"Oh, Sherlock, you're helping that poor splotchy woman?" my grandma says, entering the room. "I'm so proud of you," she coos, and kisses me on the cheek.

"What about me?" Hailey protests. "What am I? A throw pillow over here?" Grandma gives her a peck on the cheek, too.

Grandma points out the photo's highlights. "That's Mrs. Bagby in her pre-splotch days, that is her unpleasantly hairy boyfriend

Bobby, and this is the artist McGuffin, and that is the painting that's been stolen. She said this photo is over thirty-five years old, but it's the only one she has of the painting."

"It helps, Grandma," I say, staring at the photo. "It proves that Mrs. Bagby got the painting directly from the artist himself, and it will go a long way in proving that it's authentic. That is, of course, if we ever see it again."

"Ah, there's the rub," Hailey says, shooting me a look.

"I need an art expert right now," I announce. "Is Jessie home?"

"She's home, dear," Grandma says, looking down the hallway. "But she's not in a very good mood."

I start off down the hallway, into the jaws of the beast. "Well, at least there's something I can count on in this world," I say to nobody in particular.

• Chapter 13 •
A Closed-Door Policy

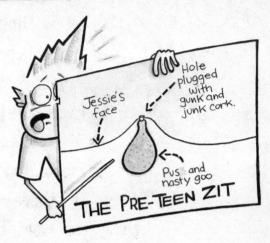

Jessie's face

Hole plugged with gunk and junk cork.

Pus and nasty goo

THE PRE-TEEN ZIT

My sister is the artist in my family. I've flipped through all her secret notebooks full of her sketches, drawings, and watercolors. And she has more art books than most libraries. Plus, Jessie's so miserable and grouchy that she's sure to become a successful artist one day.

But she won't open her bedroom door.

"Go away, you worm!" Jessie snaps from

behind the door. This is not like her; she usually prefers to fling her door open and yell at me face-to-face— she loves the personal touch.

"Is there some-thing you want to talk about?" I shout at the door, knowing that this question will irritate her tremendously.

She's quiet for a moment. "My life is over," she warbles.

Oh, no. Whenever my sister says this, it means she has a zit.

In case you don't already know, a zit is basically a clogged hole in your face's skin. The hole plugs up with gunk, grease, and grime so bad that it forms a tiny cork. Meanwhile, a little pink volcano of pus and nasty goo builds up underneath the whole mess.

"I'm sure it's not so bad," I say through the door, hearing a ticking clock in the back of my mind. "I bet I don't even notice it."

With that Jessie's door unlocks with a snap and the door swings open with a big gust of wind. "Notice anything unusual?" she growls.

"Wow!" I say, my mouth dropping open in amazement. "It looks like you're growing another head through your nose."

"I told you!" she thunders.

"Has it said anything yet?" I ask, unable to take my eyes off the massive lump. "Can you even see straight?"

"My life is over," she says, looking up at the ceiling.

"Hey, I'm not here to take photos," I say as

calmly as I can. "I'm here to ask some questions about an artist. It's for a case I'm—"

"Oh my gosh, Jessie!" Hailey wails from just inches behind my right ear. "You're growing some kind of a horn out of the side of your beak!"

Her timing could not have been worse. Before I can stop Jessie, she slams her door and crawls back into her shell like a zitty, moody hermit crab.

"Thanks a lot," I grumble, not turning around.

"Forget the Pimple Princess," Hailey says with a wave.

"I HEARD THAT!" comes a shrill scream from behind the door.

"The phone's been hopping," she says, tapping me on the shoulder with the cell phone. "We've got some hot leads, Sherlock. So zip up your zipper and let's get to work."

"Not again!" I snap, zipping up that dang, low-flying fly.

I'm not sure what leads Hailey's referring to, but when your ship is sinking fast, you'll grab on to just about anything.

"I still need Jessie's help," I say, looking at the artist in the photo.

"Forget it," Hailey says. "Unless you can bribe her."

Then I remember something. "I can't bribe her, but I can blackmail her." I slowly pull the crumbled index cards from my back pocket. The list of boys Jessie thinks are cute didn't help me with my Sherlock Holmes report, but they'll be perfect for convincing Jessie to help us.

Hey, nobody said this business was pretty.

• Chapter 14 •
The Slow Boat to Baskerville

"Grandma, is this as fast as your car goes?"

I'm in a near panic in the backseat of my grandma's car. We're heading back downtown. I just hope we make it before the holiday season gets here.

"Are you in some kind of energy-saving gear?"

Luckily, my grandma refuses to drive in Bessie, the car heard round the world, which my grandpa is still trying to bring back to life in front of Lance's house. Grandma insists on driving her own car. I can't say I blame her; my ears are still ringing.

Hailey is sitting next to me, plowing through a book about meat-eating plants—she must have finished the book about shipwrecks when I wasn't looking.

Jessie is sitting silently up front with our grandma. I'd probably be able to see steam coming out of her ears, but she has a towel draped over her head. She doesn't want to be seen in her current state of zittiness.

"So what's with this artist Arthur McGuffin?" I ask the towel. "How come there are only forty-three of his paintings in existence?"

"AAAAGH!" the towel snarfs. "He burned most of his paintings in a fit of rage one night. I know how he felt. So is that it? Can I have

those cards back now, you little thief?"

"Not so fast," I say. Boy, she sounds touchy. "Do you think this McGuffin guy could have stolen his painting to burn it?"

"He's been dead for over twenty years, so I think you can rule him out as a suspect."

"You're probably right," I say quietly.

I watch out the window as a kid on a skateboard blows past us like we're standing still. "Grandma, I think I can do a crab walk faster than this."

"Don't rush me, honey," she says, coasting to a very gradual stop at the corner of Baker Street and Conan Avenue.

Like most old people I've encountered, my grandma hates to be rushed. Apparently, once you're old enough to grow hair out of your ears, the concept of rushing around to accomplish things suddenly seems pointless and ridiculous.

"Have you ever heard of the painting in this photo?" I ask the towel. "It's called *Man with a Cat*."

Jessie growls from under the towel. "I didn't know the name of it, no. Nobody does. It was always just a rumor."

"And this artist is all famous and stuff?"

"I can't believe this!" she snips. "Yeah, he's 'all famous and stuff.' He's only the most famous and influential artist from this region ever, so there'd be lots of interest if a new painting of his turned up."

"So it's worth a lot of money?" I ask.

"More money than you'll make in a

lifetime," she snarks. She holds out her hand and snaps her fingers.

"I'm still thinking of questions," I inform her.

Officer Lestrade told Hailey he'd meet us at the mayor's mansion. He'll be on his coffee break, since his chief ordered him not to log in any more time on the theft of a painting that might not be worth a darn.

The chief might change his mind if he saw Mrs. Bagby's photo.

Clem, the maintenance guy at the museum, told Hailey that the museum was closed yesterday but the entire city council toured it late in the afternoon. And although he couldn't be sure, Clem thought Mayor Fliggle was the last one to come down the stairs. He remembered because the mayor was wearing cowboy boots, and they made a colossal racket coming down the stairs.

And no, Clem didn't remember hearing any

OUR MAYOR
ROBERT P. FLIGGLE

breaking glass.

Hailey had called City Hall, but the mayor and his boots had already skipped out for the day. She was somehow able to talk us into an emergency meeting at the mayor's mansion, which is right next to City Hall. I don't ask how she was able to accomplish this—I don't think I want to know.

I'm just hoping the mayor noticed something yesterday. Or saw somebody fishy hanging around. Or even remembers if the painting was still hanging on the wall!

I realize he is my best shot, because tracking down and interviewing the entire city council could take days.

So many leads, so little time.

I watch all the other traffic on the road whiz past us. "Would it help if I got out and pushed, Grandma?"

Not surprisingly, Lance isn't helping much. He had called when we were rolling away from the house. He and Jimmy Chee burned a batch of cookies, the smoke alarm went off, and he got sidetracked opening all the windows in his house. I'm secretly pleased the sleepover isn't going so splendidly, but I need Lance to get to work.

As we finally exceed tricycle speed on the Baskerville Expressway, the cell phone rings.

Hailey drops her book about flesh-eating flowers, and answers. She listens quietly and says, "Okay, thanks, Clem."

She snaps the phone shut, looks at me, and goes back to her book.

"Well?" I say in exasperation.

"That was Clem," she says without looking up. "He said the auction has started. The first two paintings have already sold and the crowd is bidding on number three."

I look up hopefully as the car comes to a sudden stop, which isn't easy to detect when your average speed doesn't exceed slow and slower.

But we're not in front of the mayor's mansion!

We're stopped on the off-ramp to downtown. It looks like a parking lot! With panic rising in my throat like a plate of bad clams, I figure we're still five city blocks from where I should have been two hours ago.

I can either cry or do something dramatic.

Or cry dramatically, of course.

Instead, I open my door and jump out.

"What about my cards!" Jessie shrieks from under the towel.

"I'll meet you at City Hall!" I shout, slam the door before they can tell me that I've gone crazy, and rocket off between the honking cars.

Before I know it, the wind is in my face, downtown Baskerville is spread out before me, and I'm running so fast I can't figure out why I don't wear a cape.

I was not only blessed with a natural gift for solving mysteries, I was given the gift of speed.

I'm likely to be the biggest star the Baskerville junior track team has ever had— once I'm no longer suspended from the team. (Coach Lowney gave me some time off to "pull my head out of the sand" after I kept forgetting about our track meets and practices.)

But track team or not, the madness of downtown Baskerville on this Friday evening is whizzing past me like I've been fired out of a king-size slingshot. I can tell from the cool breeze that my lazy zipper is down again, but I simply can't afford to stop and deal with another wardrobe malfunction.

I'm making great speed, but my mind is racing even faster.

I'm haunted by the image of the sad-looking hole in the auction room's wall, the broken glass sprinkled in the alley, and the curator's massive noggin. I even gag reflexively two or three times at the memory of my favorite shirt.

Have I missed something? Is this too much for one kid to handle? Do I need a license to run this fast?

I easily pass a guy delivering a stack of pizzas on the back of his motorized scooter— *my growling stomach almost has a heart attack!* I am nearly pancaked by a lady swerving all over the road while blabbing on two cell phones at the same time. And I narrowly avoid crushing myself like an accordion against a taxi door that suddenly pops open.

It's crazy, but it feels like it's all my fault that Mrs. Bagby's treasured masterpiece has been stolen. I feel terrible, like I've let her down. I've never encountered a case that I wasn't able to crack, but my winning streak may be coming to an abrupt and ugly end. The frustration fuels my legs to churn even faster.

As my pounding thighs carry me up the polished stairs of the mayor's mansion, I know I've run five city blocks in less than four minutes—it must be a record! But more importantly, I'm feeling more determined than ever to ride the final drop of this roller-coaster ride to the bitter end.

I'm about to take the slim prayer I have of solving this case for every cent it's worth.

• Chapter 16 •
You Can't Fight City Hall

Mayor Robert P. Fliggle lives in a swanky mayor's residence that itself could be called a museum.

I must admit, I'm impressed.

And disgusted. Our school's science lab has only five microscopes—three are broken and the other two don't work! Meanwhile, our mayor lives like a fat cat in bird heaven.

After I've been pacing around like a caged

shark for five long minutes, an aide ushers me down the hall to the mayor's home office. I notice that all the art hanging on the walls looks pricey. It appears as if Baskerville's mayor is something of an art lover himself, so getting his cooperation may not be so hard after all.

In my head, I try to calculate how many microscopes one of these paintings would buy. I reach a grand total: plenty.

I'm turned loose in the mayor's office.

Mayor Fliggle is on the phone, leaning back in his chair, boots up on his desk. Although he certainly looks fat and happy, he seems smaller in person than he looks on TV. I imagine that's common with politicians.

He holds his hand over the phone. "Your zipper's down, son."

"I know," I say, irritated at my impossible situation.

He looks confused for half a second. "Trying to start a new fashion trend, eh?" He says this with a rumbling chuckle and a shake of his head. "Nice shirt, too." He pulls his hand from the phone. "Twenty-three five," he says into the phone, and gives me a thumbs-up sign.

"I'm here about my art teacher's painting. It was stolen from the museum last night."

The mayor picks up a slip of paper off his desk. "It says here you needed an emergency

meeting because you have three million dollars you'd like to donate to my next campaign."

"I did?" I croak. "Oh! No, that's just my sister. I mean, that was her idea. I'm here about the stolen painting."

The mayor seems puzzled by the sudden change in his agenda.

"Yes! A shame! A scandal!" he says to me, staring at the note again. "Twenty-four," he says into the phone. "The newspaper keeps calling me for a comment," he says to me, or to someone on the phone—it's getting hard to tell.

"Did you notice anything unusual when you were in the museum yesterday?" I ask, feeling my chances fading by the second.

"Who are you again?" he says, giving me a sideways glance.

"I've been hired to recover my art teacher's painting," I say.

"Are you putting me on?" he says, forcing a smile. "Is this a joke? A prank? Is there someone out in the hall?"

"I'm no prank, although many people think I'm a joke," I say, instantly kicking myself for saying something so lame. I'm not even sure what I mean by it. I wish my mouth would just keep its mouth shut!

"But there *is* someone out in the hall!"

It's Hailey. She's out in the hall. Finally, she's announced herself before sneaking up on me. Miracles really *do* happen.

"Sherlock, I need to talk to you!" she hisses from the hallway, refusing to enter the room.

"Just a minute," I hiss back.

"Twenty-five five," the mayor says into the phone, not sure if the drama that's playing out in front of him is a comedy or a tragedy.

"Right now!" Hailey whispers urgently. "You need to hear what I have to say."

"Great! I'll pick it up tomorrow," the mayor says. "Send me a bill."

"Me?" I say, confused.

"No, not you," he says. "Look, I'm not even sure who you are!"

"It's complicated," I say, backing out of the room. "Um, hold on, Mister Mayor, er . . . Your Honor . . . I've got to talk to my little sister for a second."

"Is she the one with the three million dollars?" he asks, throwing his arms up in the air with confusion.

"Lance called," Hailey whispers in my ear. "The mayor's name is Robert."

"You're interrupting me to tell me who I'm talking to?" I growl between clenched teeth. "I know that already!"

"Granted, you have an uncanny grasp of the completely obvious, Sherlock," she says, grabbing me by the shoulders. "But do you know the mayor's nickname?"

"How should I know? Is it Fat Cat? Mayor Big Booty?"

"I heard that!" the mayor calls out from behind his desk.

"People named Robert are often called Bob," Hailey whispers. "And sometimes they're called Bobby."

"And?"

"Remember Mrs. Bagby's boyfriend?" she says, pulling the photo from my back pocket and pointing to the hairy guy with Mrs. Bagby.

"So they have the same name!" I exclaim. "That doesn't mean anything. It could just be—"

"I called Mrs. Bagby," Hailey interrupts, waving the cell phone in my face. "She confirmed that the mayor was her boyfriend, the one in the picture, when the artist gave

WHAT HAPPENED?

MAYOR FLIGGLE **THEN**

MAYOR FLIGGLE **NOW**

her that painting. They broke up not long after that. She hasn't spoken two words to the mayor since then. It didn't end well."

"But that doesn't mean he stole the painting," I argue, trying to see the mayor in the bearded guy in the photo.

"That's not all," Hailey says, checking the hallway for anybody who may be listening. "Lance also told me who the museum's chairman is. . . ."

My eyes open wide. A tingle creeps over my scalp like a tarantula on roller skates. I'm hearing bells and whistles and sirens in my head. "The mayor?" I croak.

Hailey nods. "That means something, right? The mayor was the one telling the curator to get rid of us and sweep this mess under the rug."

"Why didn't Mrs. Bagby say anything about the mayor?"

"She didn't know he was mixed up in this," she says.

Like a key sliding into a lock, the tumblers in my head click into place. I feel like a drowning man who just got hit on the head with a lifeline. A ray of hope breaks through the darkness inside my skull. I run for the light.

"It means something, all right," I say slowly. "It means we need to go now."

"Go?" Hailey shrieks. "Go where? We've got the mayor right where we want him. Let's go in there and squeeze him like a kitchen sponge!"

"Mayor Fliggle, this meeting is over!" I announce, and start pulling Hailey back down the hall.

"What about the donation?" the mayor hollers from his office. "I don't need all three million at once!"

I now know that Mayor Fliggle knows all about Mrs. Bagby and her treasured masterpiece. As the museum chairman, the mayor is also aware of all of the ins and outs of the museum. He even appears to like nice paintings. But does that mean he stole *Man with a Cat*?

I'm the only one who can crack this case, but I'm still only half cracked at this point! And once the auction is over, my instincts tell me my chances of solving this mystery will be, too.

It's clear that the next few minutes will either whisk me directly into a glorious hero's welcome or smack dab into an extra-thick brick wall.

• Chapter 17 •
Rolling Code Eleven

When we explode out of the front door of the mayor's mansion, I don't see my grandma's car anywhere. She's probably circling the block, so she'll swing by again sometime around sunrise.

I consider trying to sprint across town to the museum but don't want to leave Hailey in the dust—she may be smart, but she runs like ten pots and pans tied together with kite string.

Then I see Officer Lestrade sitting in his cruiser at the curb! That's two miracles in a row! They say these things happen in threes!

I grip Hailey under my arm and carry her like a football as fast as I can to the police cruiser. It must look like I've just stolen a very short scarecrow.

"I can't breathe, you nutcase," she wheezes, trying to pry my arm loose.

I throw open the rear door of the police cruiser and toss Hailey inside like a sack of turnips. I dive in after her.

We bump our heads so hard I see stars and fairy dust everywhere.

"You two scared the wits out of me!" Officer Lestrade hollers.

"Quick, get us to the museum as fast as you can!" I demand, as the stars turn into floating walnuts.

"What? Why?" Officer Lestrade yelps,

surely taken aback by my wild eyes.

"I'm half cracked," I wail, smashing my nose on the bulletproof glass while smearing a streak of slobber on it for good measure.

For a split second, I can't remember who I am or why I've been arrested.

Hailey smashes her nose on the glass next to mine. "Roll code eleven, Officer Lestrade. We've only got minutes. Sherlock knows where the painting is!"

"HE DOES?" Officer Lestrade shouts.

"I DO?" I wail directly into Hailey's face.

"YOU MEAN YOU DON'T?" Hailey shouts back.

But there isn't time for me to answer. Officer Lestrade throws the cruiser into such a sudden and powerful U-turn that I think for a moment that the world has come to an end.

Hailey comes flying at me. The force of the turn is so great that the weight of Hailey's

body squeezes what little air I have from my lungs. I think one of her fingers is in my eye, or it's one of mine—I can't tell in all the confusion.

I can hear the shrill squeal of tires grabbing the street.

Because of the blow to my head, I can hear bells and sirens again— No, that's the cruiser's siren and the cell phone ringing.

"I CANT FIND THE PHONE!" Hailey shrieks,

searching with her hands for the phone.

The engine roars. The siren wails. The lights flash. The cars part in front of us. I could get used to this!

"WHERE'S THE PAINTING?" Officer Lestrade thunders.

"IT'S NOT THAT SIMPLE!" I shout through the glass.

"CAN I CALL YOU BACK WITH AN UPDATE IN TEN MINUTES, MRS. BAGBY?" Hailey pleads into the phone.

"WHAT? YOU ONLY HAVE AN INK-LING?" Hailey screams at me.

"SOMETHING LIKE THAT!" I shout back.

"YOU DON'T KNOW WHAT AN INKLING IS, DO YOU?"

"NOT EXACTLY!"

"I CAN GET IN TROUBLE FOR USING MY SIREN WITHOUT A LEGITIMATE REASON!"

"OH, THIS IS LEGITIMATE, ALL RIGHT!" I thunder, although I don't have the foggiest idea what the word "legitimate" means.

As we weave in and out of traffic, my old friend carsickness stops by for a visit. My stomach inflates with nauseousness. My throat tightens up. My neck is stiff and sweaty. I thank my lucky stars I haven't eaten lately—that's not much for a third miracle, but I'll take it.

A DANGEROUSLY INFLATED STOMACH

It's all I can do to ask Hailey to call Clem.

The traffic thins out as we approach the museum, and Officer Lestrade turns off the siren but keeps his lights flashing.

"Clem, it's me!" Hailey finally says into the phone. "Is it over? What?" She turns to me. "They're still bidding on the last painting. What do you want me to ask him?"

"Ask him if the mayor bought anything," I gasp, clutching my belly.

She does.

"No, the mayor hasn't bid on anything, as far as he knows. But he says that there are lots of anonymous bidders on the phone." Hailey can read my face better than Miss Piffle. "'Anonymous' means you don't know who they are."

"Oh," I say, the wheels spinning wildly in my head, desperate for anything to grab on to. I think of something. "Ask him if a painting sold

for exactly twenty-five five. That's the last number the mayor said on the phone in his office. That could have been a winning bid, as in twenty-five thousand five hundred dollars."

"WHO CARES IF HE BOUGHT A PAINTING!"

"JUST ASK HIM!"

She asks, and I wait. The seconds drag on. I quietly hope the "not eating in the last few hours" thing wasn't my last miracle. I need another one.

"Okay, thanks, Clem," Hailey says, and snaps the phone shut. "Clem says a big red painting called *Untitled Number 14* just sold for exactly twenty-five thousand five hundred dollars to an unknown bidder on the phone."

"That must be the worst name for a painting ever," I cry, just as Officer Lestrade whips the cruiser to the curb in front of the museum.

"Why's that interesting?" Hailey croaks. "How's that help?"

"I gotta go," I say.

When Office Lestrade finally opens my door, I explode out of the car and race up the steps to the museum.

"WAIT!" they both call after me. But I don't have time for small talk.

I'm about to make a fool of myself, or save the day. The odds are not in my favor. But I'm always willing to bet it all on a long shot.

• Chapter 18 •
Madman on the Loose!

When I burst into the crowded auction room and stumble up the middle aisle, the entire crowd jumps to its feet and lets out a gasp of alarm, as if a werewolf with bloody fangs has crashed their party.

"Where's *Untitled Number 14?*" I gasp between rapid breaths.

The well-dressed crowd just stares at me, not believing what they're seeing.

"Isn't he a little old for an Inspector Wink-Wink shirt?" somebody whispers.

"And why is his zipper down?" someone else adds.

"Does anyone have a net?" a man calls out nervously.

At the front of the room I see Stone Head. He's standing at the microphone at the front of the room. He's holding a large wooden hammer, probably for just such an occasion.

"Do I look that bad?" I ask the man who asked for the net. He nods uncertainly.

"Maybe he just got hit by a car," a woman says, pointing. "His eyes look like glazed donuts."

"They do?" I croak.

Stone Head pushes his way through the crowd. "This is most unusual! Sherlock, isn't it?" He starts circling me. He's got a wooden hammer, and I've got nothing but a broken zipper. "We're here to help you," he says.

I've seen enough movies to know that when someone says this, it means you're about to be pounced on and beaten like a rented mule.

So I make a run for it.

The next minute is complete chaos.

The crowd shrieks. Chairs are overturned. Several men join the chase. But none of them has my kind of speed.

I sprint around the outside of the room. The paintings whiz by my face. I glance at the name on each sticker under each painting as it

flies by: *Flight of Fancy. Somber Night. Eternal Embrace.*

Where the heck is *Untitled Number 14*?

I'm forced to zigzag through several men who try to catch me in their coats like I'm some kind of runaway chimp. They've obviously never seen a chimp as fast as me.

Then I see it. *Untitled Number 14*! I stop short and grab the huge painting's frame to help me regain my balance. The immense painting swings wildly on the wall with a loud scraping sound.

The crowd lets out a cry.

"Is there a zookeeper in the house?" somebody shouts.

Realizing that a mob is closing in fast, I lift the painting away from the wall, reach up with my free hand, and unhook *Man with a Cat* from its hiding place behind *Untitled Number 14*, where it hangs on its own hook. I hold up all twelve-by-twenty-two inches for everyone to see.

The crowd surrounding me gasps at the painting's unexpected appearance.

But nobody looks as surprised, or as pleased, as Stone Head. From the emotion that registers on his rocklike features, I know that he had nothing to do with this "vanishing" masterpiece.

"You found it," Stone Head says, breaking into what must be a rare smile. "You really did it."

"And he has a photo that proves it's a true

Artie McGuffin masterpiece," Hailey says, squeezing into the circle of bodies.

"But who hid it behind there?" Stone Head asks, his eyes burning.

I hesitate, unsure about how much I should reveal. The thought of speaking in front of this many people makes me dizzy. My mouth feels like it's full of sand. My legs feel like noodles. I'd faint right now if I knew how.

"Great work, Sherlock," I hear Officer Lestrade's voice call out from somewhere in the back of the room.

Somebody starts clapping. And soon the room explodes with nervous laughter, applause, and calls of "Bravo!"

As I hand the painting over to Stone Head, I know it will surely be the night's most popular auction item.

It's a moment that would make even Sherlock Holmes jealous.

"What happened in there?" Hailey asks.

"I squeezed him like a kitchen sponge," I laugh.

We're standing outside the doors of the mayor's mansion. I've just completed a tense follow-up meeting with Mayor Fliggle. I wave down to Officer Lestrade, who's waiting at the curb in his cruiser.

"Why don't we have Officer Lestrade

arrest the mayor right now?" Hailey asks.

"Well, technically the mayor didn't steal anything," I sigh. "He just moved something out of sight. It never left the room. He probably planned to move it out of the building secretly when he picked up *Untitled Number 14*."

"He admitted he moved the painting?"

"Not until I asked to see the heels of his boots," I say, smiling. "There were a half dozen perfectly round dents in the heel of his right boot, which I'm sure match the size of the nail holding the missing hook. He moved the hook, then used his boot as a hammer."

"How'd you figure that out?" she asks.

THE BOOT HAMMER!

"Well, it just never made sense that an art thief would need to steal a hook. I should have thought more about the missing hook when we first got to the museum. He must have broken the window with his boot, too, so everyone would think the painting was gone. Pretty clever."

"So our mayor's a thief?" Hailey asks, shocked by the idea.

"Well, he *is* a politician," I observe. "Of course, he claims that the artist, McGuffin, actually gave that painting to him, not to Mrs. Bagby. They argued about it at the time, and it eventually led to their breakup. I guess this was his opportunity to get back what he thought was always his."

"I can't even picture the two of them in the same room."

"It was a long time ago," I conclude with a shrug. "I guess hard feelings last a lifetime.

He says he eventually would have split the money with her, but I doubt it."

"So we're just letting him go?"

"Not exactly. I agreed not to tell my whole story to the *Baskerville Daily News* on the condition that he did three things."

Hailey waits. "Do you want me to start guessing?"

I start down the steps for Officer Lestrade's cruiser. "The mayor is going to pass an emergency funding bill next week. The Baskerville police department will soon have plenty of money for new equipment, the cameras in the museum will finally get hooked up, and the science lab at our school will soon have thirty new microscopes."

"Not bad, Sherlock," Hailey says, clearly impressed. "Now let's go celebrate with some flat-rabbit stew."

Now that Mrs. Bagby has gobs of money for

a fabulous retirement, and since the mayor has promised to stick to the terms of our agreement, I plan to honor my end of the deal and keep the details of this case quiet. I do, however, plan to use the index cards in my pocket to persuade Jessie to help me write a new oral report on a famous artist named Arthur McGuffin. I bet it makes Miss Piffle's eyebrow dance a jig.